First there was grass, then flowers, then trees, then animals, and last men and women; and this is how it came to be.

MOON MOTHER

A NATIVE AMERICAN CREATION TALE

Adapted and illustrated by

ED YOUNG

WILLA PERLMAN BOOKS
AN IMPRINT OF HARPERCOLLINS PUBLISHERS

THE EARTH was very beautiful; there was
no cold; it was summer always. Grass, flowers,
and trees covered the face of the earth; there
were lakes and rivers.

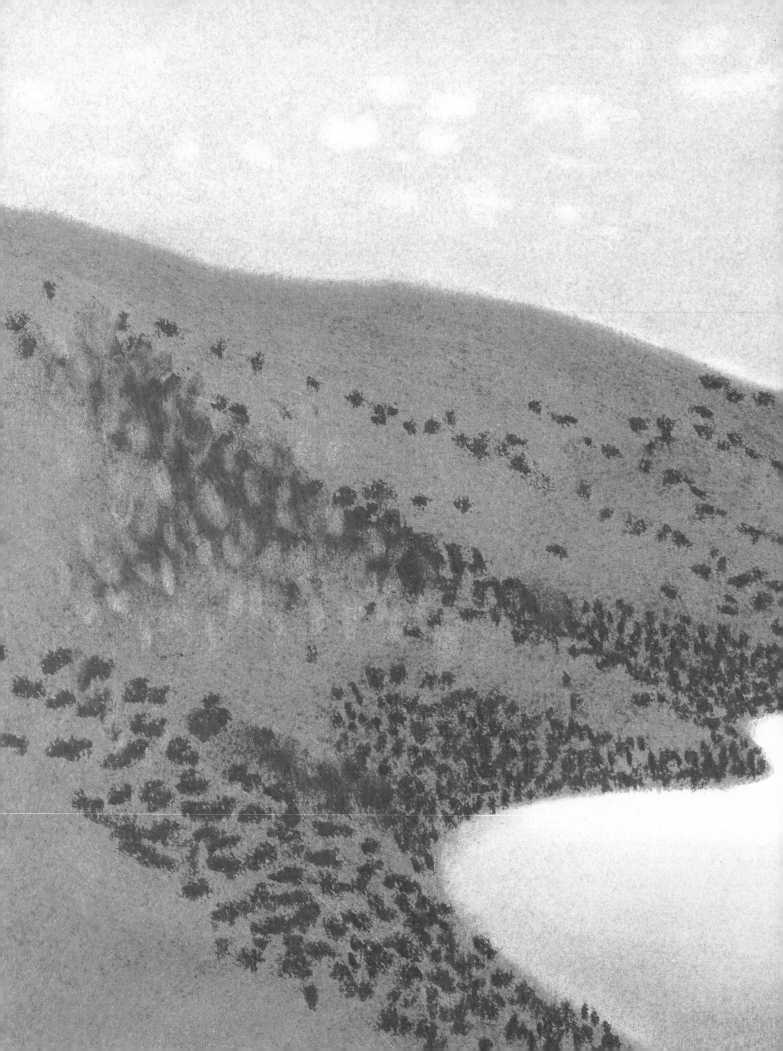

There were nuts, fruits, roots, and berries, but there was no one to eat them. Then a spirit person saw this beautiful place and said, "I will live here." But soon he became very lonesome, so he amused himself by making the animals.

He made the fishes and taught them to swim.
He made the birds and taught them to fly.

He made the foxes, coyotes, bears, raccoons,
squirrels, deer, and all animals, and taught them
how to live.

After a time he tired of his creatures and of
making new animals. He longed for some friends
and companions.

Therefore he made images of himself, and warmed them and made them alive; and this is how men came to be.

He talked with the men and taught them how to make spears, bows, arrows, and knives. He showed them how to weave blankets, build houses, make fire, and how to roast their food and burn clay to make pots.

Then the animals complained to the spirit person that his new creatures hunted and slew them, so to each he gave some protection against the men. The skunk had been his pet and was very tame, so to him he gave the surest safeguard of all.

In this manner the spirit person and the men lived very happily for a long time; but after a time there came out of the sky another spirit person, a woman, and she lived near a lake in a beautiful valley. It was not very long until the first spirit person found the woman spirit person, and, because she was of his own kind, he remained with her.

Then the men went to him and said, "Have you forgotten us?" But he said, "Do as I have taught you, and the earth will care for you."

But the men began to quarrel and fight among themselves. Finally, one man by his bravery, strength, and quickness became chief among the men; and he said, "Come, let us go to our good friend." So they went together to the house of the spirit people, but they had gone away, and in the silence the men were awestruck and dared not go farther.

The chief went forward, when there came a
wail from inside the sacred house that chilled
their blood, and great fear seized their hearts.

The chief was courageous, as a chief ought
to be. He went to the sacred house, and there
upon the threshold lay a newborn girl baby.
The spirit people had gone, but they had left
a gift for the men.

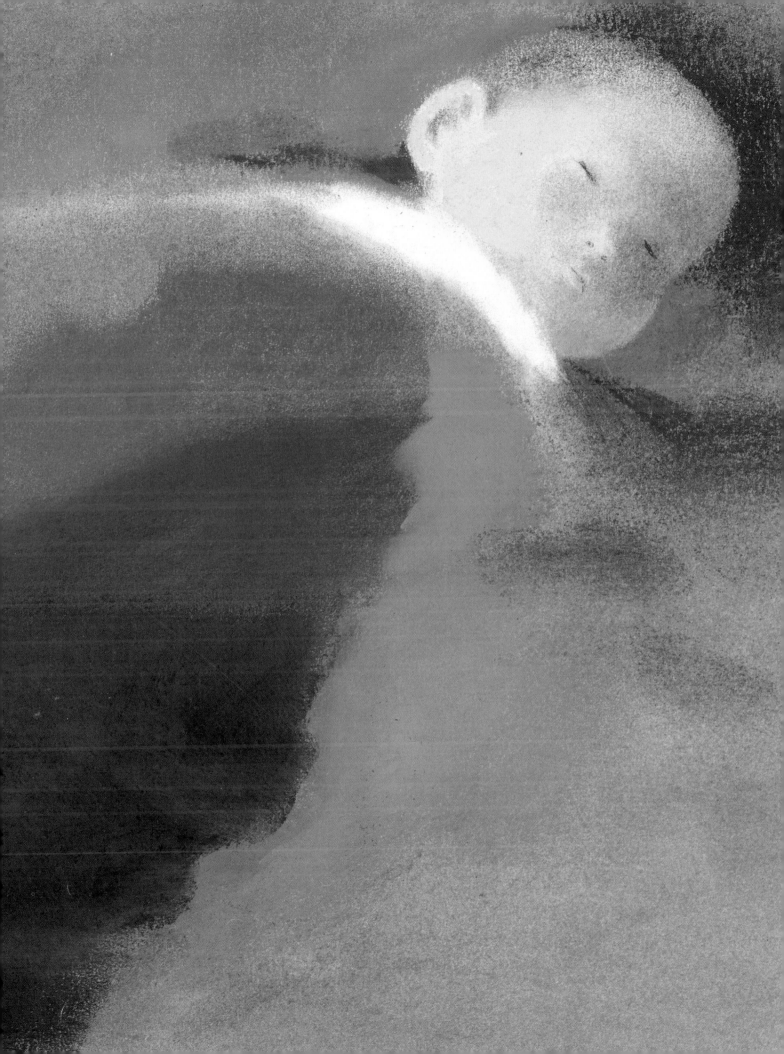

And when the night came, there was a new
light in the sky, and the men saw that the moon
was the face of the woman spirit person, who is
carried across the sky every night by her husband,
that she may play with the stars. The chief took
the baby to his house, and all the men waited
upon her.

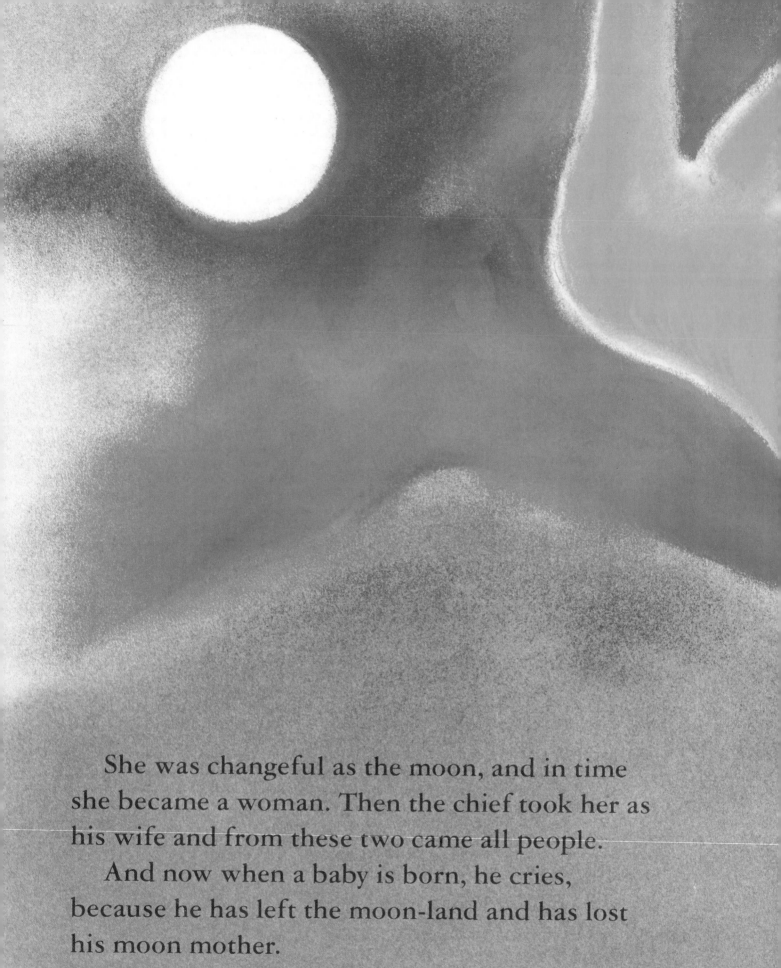

She was changeful as the moon, and in time
she became a woman. Then the chief took her as
his wife and from these two came all people.
    And now when a baby is born, he cries,
because he has left the moon-land and has lost
his moon mother.

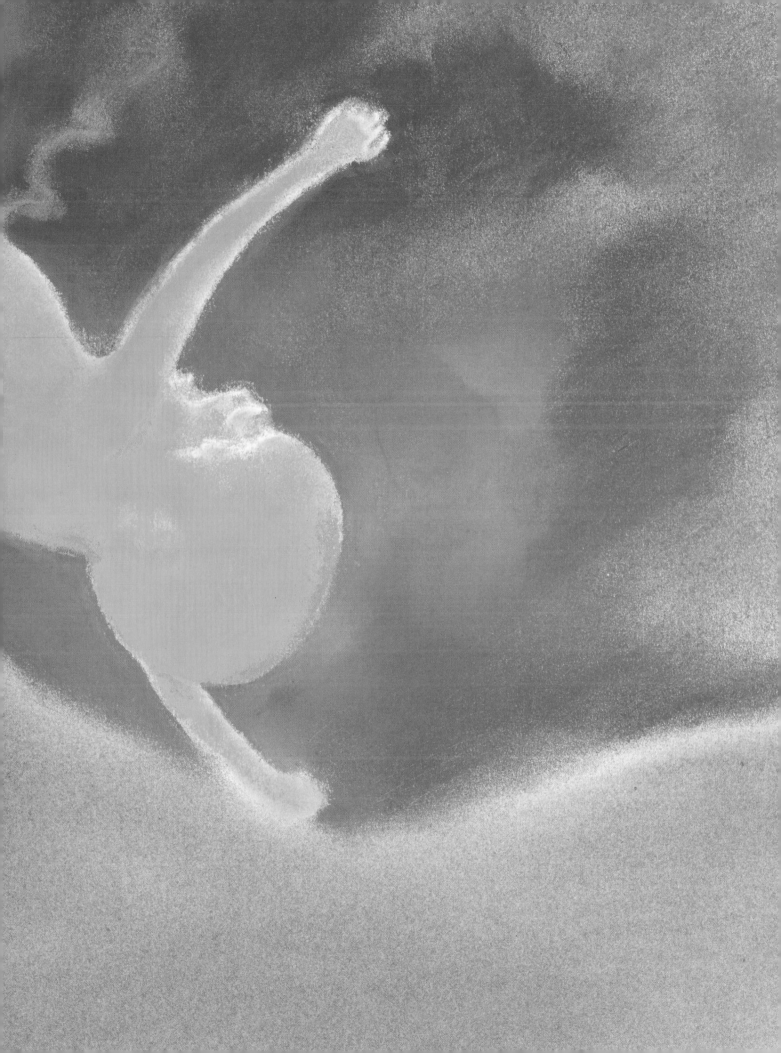

And when one is old and feeble, he dies when the moon mother's face is turned away from him.